SpongeBob gasped. The lightbulb that hung above the class science project, Roger, had crackled and burned out. The room was dim.

SpongeBob looked at Patrick. Then he looked at Roger. Then he looked at Patrick again. If SpongeBob and Patrick didn't act fast, Roger could die!

"I-I-I'm sorry I called you a stupid star!" SpongeBob cried.

"I'm sorry I got you into trouble, and got you moved to the back of the room, and got your Good Noodle star taken away, and threw a book at you, and shot spitballs at you, and . . . ," Patrick babbled anxiously.

"I'm sorry your apology is so long!" SpongeBob interrupted.

"Me too!" said Patrick.

Their eyes locked. "Let's save Roger!"

NEW Student

STARFISH

NEW STUDENT STARFISH

by Jenny Miglis

illustrated by Heather Martinez

Simon Spotlight/Nickelodeon

New York   London   Toronto   Sydney   Singapore

Stephen Hillenburg

Based on the TV series *SpongeBob SquarePants*®
created by Stephen Hillenburg as seen on Nickelodeon®

SIMON SPOTLIGHT
An imprint of Simon & Schuster Children's Publishing Division
1230 Avenue of the Americas, New York, New York 10020

Manufactured in the United States of America

First Edition
2 4 6 8 10 9 7 5 3 1

ISBN 0-689-86164-8

Library of Congress Catalog Card Number 2003101640

Look for these other
SpongeBob SquarePants
chapter books!

NEW STUDENT STARFISH

chapter one

It was a quiet morning under the sea. The residents of Bikini Bottom were all fast asleep. All except SpongeBob SquarePants.

Honk! Honk! Hoooonk! SpongeBob's foghorn alarm clock blared.

SpongeBob sprang out of bed wearing nothing but his tight, white undies and shimmied into his brown square pants.

"Time for boating school!" he said cheerfully.

The only place SpongeBob loved more than his place of employment, the Krusty Krab, was Mrs. Puff's Boating School. And while he had yet to earn his boating license, it was a small detail that didn't stop SpongeBob from trying . . . and trying and trying.

SpongeBob always passed the written exam with flying colors, but when it came to the driving test, SpongeBob got so nervous behind the wheel that he failed every time. Thirty-nine times, to be exact.

"Let her rip, Gary!" SpongeBob called out to his pet snail.

Gary slithered over to the toaster and launched a slice of toast into the air.

SpongeBob took a running leap, turned a somersault, and caught the toast with one hand. "Ta da!" He took a bow and then took a bite of the toast. "Not bad, Gary. The toast could have been a little darker though."

"Meow," Gary replied.

"See ya later!" said SpongeBob as he slid his big, blue backpack over his shoulders.

SpongeBob opened the front door to find his best friend, Patrick Star, blocking the doorway. He was holding a jellyfish net in one hand.

"Hi, SpongeBob!" Patrick said cheerfully. "Do you want to go jellyfishing?" He gave the net a practice swing.

"Sorry, Patrick. I can't," SpongeBob replied. "I have school today."

"How about a little snack at the Krusty Krab?" Patrick suggested. "I'll let you buy me a Krabby Patty."

"Tempting, but no," SpongeBob said. "I take my education very seriously. Now, if you'll excuse me . . ."

Patrick sighed, disappointed. His eyes began to well with tears. "Well, what am I supposed to do all day?" he whined.

SpongeBob shrugged. "I don't know," he said. "What do you normally do while I'm at school?"

"Oh, I just . . . well, you know, wait for you to get back," Patrick admitted sheepishly.

SpongeBob thought for a moment. "You could walk Gary for me," he suggested.

"Gee, SpongeBob, the last time I walked Gary I got lost," Patrick said. "And stung by a mob of angry jellyfish."

SpongeBob cringed remembering the welts that had covered his friend's body. "Well, you could blow bubbles," he offered. "That should be safe enough."

"Bubble blowing isn't any fun without you, SpongeBob," Patrick said wistfully. "And besides, last time I accidentally drank the bubbles and I was burping for days."

Hmmm, SpongeBob thought to himself, what can Patrick do today?

"I've got an idea!" he exclaimed. "You can come to school with me! Just think about it, Patrick, you and me . . . as classmates!"

Patrick imagined himself standing next to SpongeBob in the class picture, smiling proudly. "Wow!" cried Patrick. "This is gonna be the best day ever!"

"But first we have to find you something to wear to your first day of school," SpongeBob said. "You know what they say, 'dress for success.' You need to wear something that says, *I have arrived.*"

A few minutes later Patrick was dressed and ready to go. He was wearing a neatly pressed white shirt, a red tie, . . . and brown square pants. He looked just like SpongeBob!

"Brace yourself, Patrick," SpongeBob said. "You're in for the greatest academic thrill ride of your life!"

SpongeBob was sure this would be a day they would never forget.

chapter two

"School days, school days, dear old golden rule days . . . ," SpongeBob sang as he and Patrick approached the entrance to Mrs. Puff's Boating School. They stopped beneath a large archway.

"Well, here we are," SpongeBob said happily. "Are you ready to broaden your horizon? Expand your mind? Think out of the box?"

"Okay," Patrick said with a shrug.

SpongeBob retucked his crisp white shirt,

hiked up his square pants, and straightened his red tie. He took out his handkerchief, bent down, and gave his shiny black shoes a quick buff.

"How do I look?" SpongeBob asked Patrick.

"Uh, I dunno, yellow?" Patrick replied.

SpongeBob shook his head and tsk-tsked. "Wrong answer, my friend," he said. "I look *smart*! And so do you!"

"C'mon, Patrick," SpongeBob said as he skipped through the front gate dragging Patrick by the hand. "We don't want to be late!"

Mrs. Puff's Boating School was a small, yellow boathouse perched on a pier in front of a tall lighthouse. There was a practice track that surrounded the school where Mrs. Puff gave boating lessons to her students.

SpongeBob flung open the front doors of the school with a flourish. The hallway seemed to sparkle. The newly washed floors shone, the windows gleamed, and the walls were freshly painted. SpongeBob beamed with pride.

"Behold, Patrick, . . . the hallway of learning," SpongeBob said as he led Patrick down the long corridor lined with lockers.

SpongeBob stopped in front of the water fountain. "This, of course, is the fountain of learning," he said with awe. "I drink from it every day."

Patrick leaned in to take a drink from the fountain. He turned the knob and the water shot up, missed his open mouth, and spurted right into his eyes.

Patrick held his hands over his face. "I'm blind! I'm blind!" he cried. "I've been blinded by knowledge!"

SpongeBob took out his handkerchief and wiped Patrick's eyes. "Soak it up, buddy. Soak it up," he said and spun Patrick around. "As I was saying, these are the lockers of learning," he continued.

Patrick pointed to the staircase nearby. "Are those the stairs of learning?" he asked.

SpongeBob shrugged. "No, they're just stairs." SpongeBob scurried over to a staircase on the other side of the hallway and motioned with his arm. "*These* are the stairs of learning."

SpongeBob gave Patrick the complete tour of Mrs. Puff's Boating School: the gymnasium of learning, the lunchroom of learning, the nurse's office of learning, and even the lavatory of learning.

The two friends walked past a trophy case to a photo gallery of all of the sea folk who had earned their boating licenses at Mrs. Puff's school. The faces in the photos smiled smugly. At the end of the long row hung an empty frame with a placard that read SPONGEBOB SQUAREPANTS.

"Hey, where's your picture, SpongeBob?" Patrick wanted to know.

SpongeBob looked up at the empty frame with longing. "I have not yet made the great wall," he said sadly. "But this year I just know I'll get my boating license."

Patrick put his hand on SpongeBob's shoulder as they continued down the hallway. Patrick looked around. Mrs. Puff's Boating School seemed like an ordinary school except for one thing. The hallways were all completely empty.

"Hey, where is everybody?" Patrick wondered aloud.

"Home, I guess," SpongeBob answered. "Class doesn't start until nine o'clock."

Patrick looked at his watch and his *eyes* bulged. "It's only six twenty, SpongeBob!" he gasped. "You said *we were late!*"

SpongeBob patted his friend's back and smiled. "Late for being early, of course," he declared. "Come on, Patrick. I'll show you the room with the most *class* . . . the classroom!"

SpongeBob led Patrick to a small room at the end of the hallway. Inside there were five rows of shell-backed seats tucked into small desks in front of the teacher's desk.

There were posters of boats and navigational charts tacked on the walls. Students could practice tying nautical knots on the ropes that were tethered to the bookshelf in the back.

SpongeBob walked to the front of the room. "This is the chalkboard," he patted the board affectionately. "And like this chalkboard, we are blank slates waiting to be filled with knowledge."

"Ohhhh!" cried Patrick. "I want to be a blank slate!"

"Don't worry, Patrick," SpongeBob replied. "You are."

Next SpongeBob led Patrick to a large board filled with shiny gold stars. He looked up at it with awe.

"And this magnificent piece of work is the Good Noodle Board," SpongeBob said proudly. "Each student's name is written here," he pointed. "The gold stars next to the names are awarded for all areas of scholastic excellence: attendance, penmanship, participation, basic desk sanitation, advanced desk sanitation, et cetera. I'll write your name here, so you can start collecting stars too."

SpongeBob wrote Patrick's name neatly in

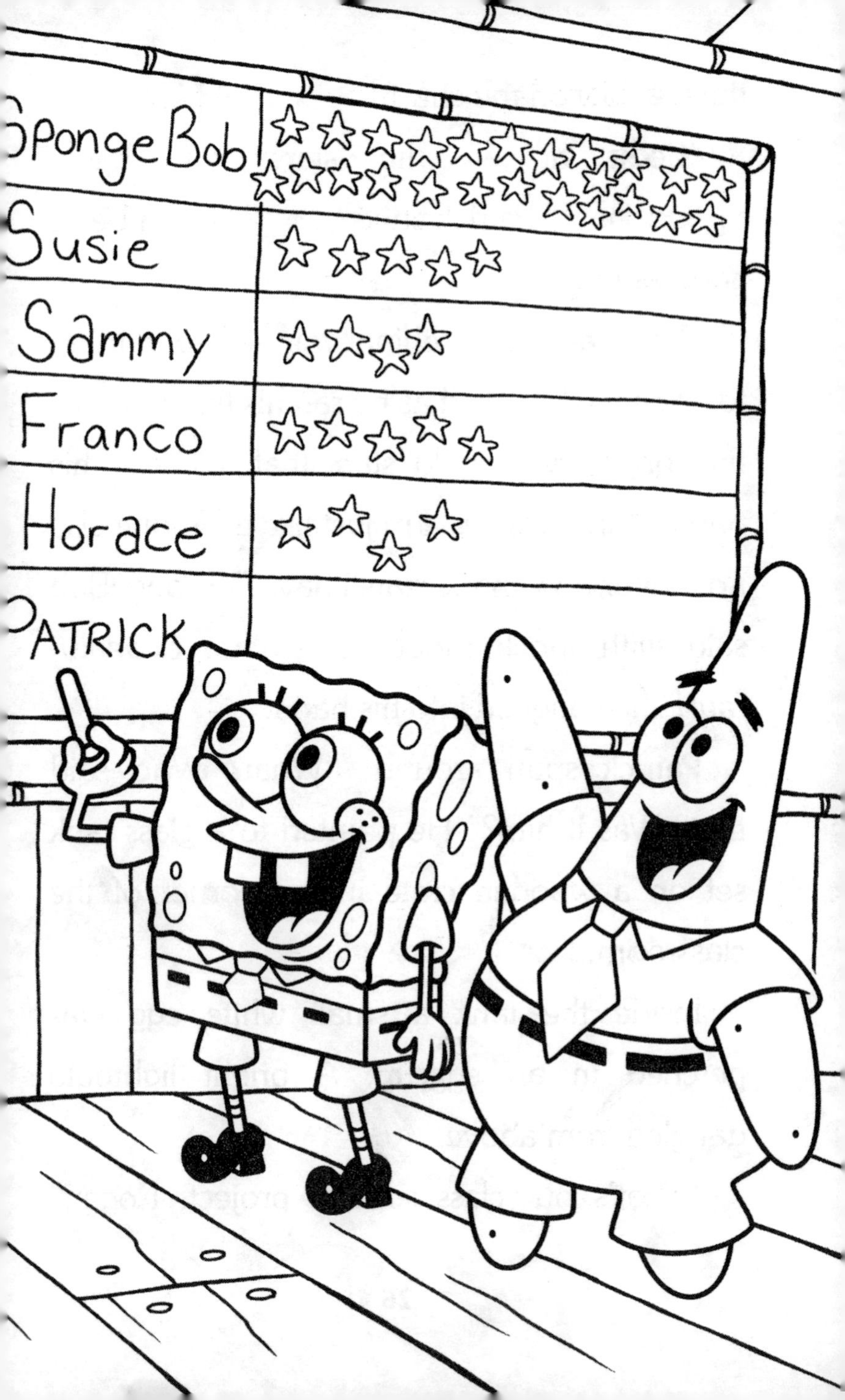
SpongeBob
Susie
Sammy
Franco
Horace
PATRICK

the last row on the chart.

"Look at all the stars you have, SpongeBob!" Patrick cried out. "I'll never be as good as you!"

"You can do anything you set your mind to," SpongeBob said as he ran his finger across the long row of gold stars that followed his name. "And besides, I'm just like everyone else no matter how many stars I have," SpongeBob said with mock modesty. "Ahem! *Seventy-four!*" he coughed into his hand.

Patrick spun around. "What? Who said that? Was it him?" He pointed to a glass tank set on a wooden crate in the corner of the classroom.

Inside the tank a small white egg was perched in an eggcup. A bright lightbulb dangled from above.

"That's our class science project, Roger,"

SpongeBob said. "He teaches us the greatest life lesson of all."

"Life's a box of chocolates?" Patrick guessed.

"No, Patrick, Roger teaches us the precious value of life," SpongeBob responded.

"Oh, right." Patrick nodded, still confused.

"You see Roger's shell represents the fragile line between life and death when behind the wheel of a boat," SpongeBob explained.

"This lightbulb represents knowledge." He paused for dramatic effect. "And without its energy and warmth, Roger would die."

Patrick switched the lightbulb on and off repeatedly. "Life! Death! Life! Death! Life! Death!" he cried with glee.

"Patrick! Stop that!" SpongeBob scolded, grabbing Patrick's hand. "If that lightbulb goes out for even a few minutes, Roger could die!

It's very important to keep him warm until he's ready to hatch."

"Hatch?! Oh, no!" cried Patrick. "Roger's going to hatch? He'll crack into a million pieces! We have to save him!"

SpongeBob rolled his eyes. "Patrick, Roger's supposed to hatch. How else will we find out what he is?"

Patrick's eyes widened. "You mean you don't already know?" he asked in disbelief. "Roger could be an alligator, or a lizard, or a terrifying sea monster!"

"Or a chick," SpongeBob suggested.

He led Patrick to a desk in front of the classroom. He pulled another one up close. "The best part about being early is that you get to sit close to the teacher."

SpongeBob took his seat right in front of Mrs. Puff's desk. "Do you think you're seaworthy enough to handle second chair?" he asked Patrick.

Patrick slid into the seat next to SpongeBob. "I'm learning!"

chapter three

At nine o'clock the students filed into Mrs. Puff's classroom. They all took seats at the far end of the room as far away from the teacher as possible.

Sammy the Shark sat next to Susie the Salmon and began to play a game of Go Fish. Franco the Flounder took out the latest comic book adventure of Mermaid Man and Barnacle Boy and began to read.

The rest of the students put their heads on

their desks and promptly dozed off.

SpongeBob took out his pencil and sharpened it to a point. Then he opened his spiral-bound notebook and turned to a clean page. Patrick did the same.

"Hello, class," said Mrs. Puff, a large spotted puffer fish wearing a red dress. "I see we have a new student today." She smiled warmly at Patrick. "Young man, please stand up and introduce yourself."

"Who's the fat kid talking to?" Patrick whispered to SpongeBob.

"She's talking to you, Patrick! She's the teacher!" SpongeBob hissed.

Mrs. Puff cleared her throat. "Excuse me, no whispering, SpongeBob. You have to set a good example for our new pupil," she said and turned to Patrick. "Go ahead, tell us your name. Don't be shy."

Patrick stood up and turned around. He stared out at the sea of blank faces. Patrick's knees began to knock together. Sweat beads formed on his upper lip and trickled down the sides of his face.

"Umm . . . umm," Patrick stammered.

He was so nervous that he couldn't remember his own name! P-P-Peter, no, that's not right, he thought. Pedro, Paco, Pierre . . . he ran down a list of names that started with the letter *p,* but none of them sounded familiar.

Then out of the corner of his eye Patrick noticed a calendar hanging on the wall. The date was the twenty-fourth of August.

"Umm . . . umm . . . my name is . . . twenty-four!" Patrick blurted out.

The students howled with laughter. Patrick just shrugged and quietly returned to his seat.

"Oh, great, another genius," Mrs. Puff mumbled under her breath. "Settle down, class," she commanded. "Today's lesson will be about how to turn a boat." Mrs. Puff began to draw a detailed diagram on the chalkboard.

SpongeBob nudged Patrick with his elbow. "Hey, Patrick, do you know what's even funnier than 'twenty-four'?" he whispered.

"No, what?" Patrick asked.

SpongeBob stifled a giggle. "Twenty-five!" he said and burst out laughing.

Patrick snorted and snickered. Then SpongeBob chuckled. Soon the two erupted in uncontrollable laughter. Patrick held his belly, guffawing loudly. SpongeBob slid onto the floor and rolled around in a fit of hysterics.

But Mrs. Puff didn't find SpongeBob and Patrick funny at all.

"Young man," she said to Patrick. "This is

your first day of school, so I'll let you off with a warning. As for you, SpongeBob, I expected more from a Good Noodle. And for someone who has failed his boating test thirty-nine times, I suggest you pay attention!"

SpongeBob hung his head, ashamed, and concentrated on copying the diagram from the chalkboard.

Patrick leaned over his desk and drew a picture. He folded it and passed it to SpongeBob. It was an unflattering drawing of Mrs. Puff. Across the top he had scrawled BIG FAT MEANIE!

"'*BIG FAT MEANIE*'?" SpongeBob read aloud. "Patrick, you can't write that about the teacher!" he scolded.

Mrs. Puff raised her eyebrows. "*What* about the teacher?" she said with a scowl. She marched over to SpongeBob's desk and snatched the picture from his hand.

"Oh, no!" SpongeBob gasped. He tried to grab the piece of paper back, but it was too late.

"Oh, my!" Mrs. Puff said with a huff. She peered at the drawing. "*As if* I really look like this!"

Mrs. Puff crumbled the paper into a ball. She narrowed her eyes and looked right at SpongeBob. Then she spun around and stomped toward the Good Noodle Board.

SpongeBob watched the scene as if it were happening in slow motion. "NOOOO!" he shrieked. He shut his eyes and covered his ears, but he could not deny what was about to happen.

Mrs. Puff glared at SpongeBob. "SpongeBob, I believe you know the punishment for two classroom disruptions," she said sourly. "Your behavior will cost you one gold star." She ripped a gold star from beside SpongeBob's name.

"Ahhhhh! No! No! No!" SpongeBob cried. He banged his fists on his desk, stood up, spun around, and then fainted onto the floor.

Patrick leaned over and slapped his friend's face. "Wake up, SpongeBob!" Patrick shouted in his ear. Startled, SpongeBob's eyelids fluttered open.

"If one wishes to be a Good Noodle, one must behave like a Good Noodle," Mrs. Puff chided.

"I am a Good Noodle! I am a Good Noodle! I am a Good Noodle!" SpongeBob chanted.

SpongeBob had always been the most earnest student at boating school, if not the most talented. He prided himself on sitting straight in his seat, paying close attention, and taking detailed notes. The loss of a gold star was a blemish on his near perfect academic record.

"You'll get your star back when you earn it," Mrs. Puff said, ignoring SpongeBob's antics and continuing her lesson. "As I was saying, the first thing you need to learn about turning a boat is . . ."

Patrick yawned. "Is it nap time yet?" he interrupted.

Mrs. Puff spun around. "SpongeBob! I've had enough of this behavior!" she shouted. "Collect your things and move to the desk in the back of the room."

SpongeBob couldn't believe his ears. "Me? B-b-but why?" he stammered.

Mrs. Puff puffed up bigger and bigger with rage. She towered over SpongeBob's desk and took a deep breath. "Because the big . . .

fat . . . meanie says so!" she boomed.

SpongeBob's skinny legs shook with fear as he slid out from behind his desk. SpongeBob's shoulders sagged and his head dropped. He turned toward the back of the room and began his long walk of shame.

When SpongeBob had almost reached the back of the room, he looked back over his shoulder at Mrs. Puff with puppy dog eyes, hoping she'd feel sorry for him and change her mind. Mrs. Puff glared back at him with 'don't-even-try-it' eyes.

"Aww, barnacles," SpongeBob sighed. "Thanks a lot, Patrick," he said as he shuffled past his friend's desk.

"Oh, you're welcome, SpongeBob!" Patrick said innocently, not knowing he had done anything wrong. "Anytime, pal!"

The back of the room was very, very far

from the front. SpongeBob could barely hear what Mrs. Puff was saying. "Yodel-ay-he-hoooooo!" SpongeBob yodeled and—*yodel-ay-he-hoo!*—his echo bounced back.

SpongeBob took his seat at an isolated desk known as skid row. The desk was dingy and decrepit and covered in graffiti. Someone had carved SKOOL IS FOR CHUMPS into the desk with a fishing hook that was still stuck there.

"What kind of student sits here?" SpongeBob worried aloud. "I-I-I guess I could still be a Good Noodle from way back here," he said hopefully, though his eyes filled with tears.

"When turning left," Mrs. Puff continued, "you must switch on your left turn signal at least forty feet from the turn, look both ways to ensure there aren't any obstacles in your path, firmly grasp the wheel, and rotate it counterclockwise . . ."

Patrick turned around in his chair. "Pssst! SpongeBob!"

SpongeBob turned his face away. Just ignore him, SpongeBob thought to himself.

Patrick ripped a piece of paper from his notebook, crumpled it into a ball, and threw it at SpongeBob. "PSSST! Hey, SpongeBob! Over here!"

Whatever you do, don't look at him, SpongeBob instructed himself. "Do-dah-do," he whistled as he twiddled his thumbs.

Patrick chewed a small bit of paper, pushed it into a straw, and blew a spitball at SpongeBob.

Whack! It landed right between SpongeBob's eyes.

No reaction.

Patrick launched another spitball that stuck to SpongeBob's long nose. And another.

And then three more.

Covered in spitballs, SpongeBob still would not look in Patrick's direction. Determined not to miss a word Mrs. Puff wrote on the chalkboard, SpongeBob wiped the sticky goo from around his eyes and continued taking notes.

Finally Patrick threw a heavy textbook that landed squarely on SpongeBob's head. "PSSSSSSSSSST! HEY, SPONGEBOB! I'M TRYING TO TELL YOU SOMETHING VERY IMPORTANT!"

"WHAT?!" SpongeBob shouted, at last.

Patrick waved. "Hi."

Just as SpongeBob was about to explode, the bell for recess rang. *BRRRRING!*

chapter four

SpongeBob stomped out of the classroom before Patrick could catch up to him. He was furious.

"Hey, buddy, wait up," Patrick called to SpongeBob. "That was some funny stuff in there! I really liked the part with the spitballs!"

SpongeBob slammed his locker door shut. "There is nothing funny about what you did, Patrick!" he yelled. "You are nothing but a speed bump on the road to higher education!" SpongeBob poked Patrick in the chest with his finger. "You got me in trouble. You got me moved to the back of the room. And, worst of all, you cost me a Good Noodle star!"

"Stars, mars. Who cares about a stupid star?" Patrick replied.

"Gee, Patrick *Star,* it seems like you would care about 'stupid stars' considering you *are* one!" SpongeBob shouted.

Patrick narrowed his eyes. "I'll deal with you after class!" he growled.

"It *is* after class!" SpongeBob growled back.

Just then the hallway filled with students. They formed a circle around SpongeBob and Patrick, chanting, "Fight! Fight! Fight!," and pumping their fins in the air.

"I don't *see* anyone fighting, do you?"

Patrick asked SpongeBob.

"They're talking about us," SpongeBob responded. "We're fighting!"

"Oh!" Patrick said. "Don't mind if I do!" He raised his fist in front of SpongeBob's face challengingly.

Patrick and SpongeBob went at it, fists flailing fast, but not touching one another at all.

"They call this a fight?" a big fish wearing a football jersey said. "This is embarrassing." The rest of the crowd murmured in agreement.

Mrs. Puff heard the commotion and hurried into the hall. "What's going on here!" she cried, pushing her way through the crowd. "Fighting?!" she exclaimed.

She picked up SpongeBob and Patrick by the backs of their pants. "Well, I can't believe

I'm saying this, but, SpongeBob SquarePants, I sentence you and your friend to . . . DETENTION . . . may Neptune have mercy on your souls!"

chapter five

SpongeBob and Patrick had been sitting in detention for one hour. There was one more hour to go. The life preserver-shaped clock ticked slowly.

Patrick was doodling his name over and over again on a scrap of paper. SpongeBob was wondering how he ended up in detention.

"In one day I've gone from a Good Noodle to a bad egg," SpongeBob said with a sigh. "And it's all Patrick's fault." He looked at his

ex-best friend who sat at a desk in the back of the room. "I hate you, Patrick!"

"I hate you more," Patrick retorted.

"I hate you no matter what!" SpongeBob said with a scowl.

"Yeah, well, I'd hate you even if I didn't hate you!" Patrick cried.

SpongeBob looked confused. "I'd hate you even if that made sense!"

"I'd hate you even if you were me!" Patrick bellowed, his face twisted in anger.

"I'd hate you even if . . . uh . . . uh . . . I'd hate you even if the lightbulb keeping Roger alive went out!" said SpongeBob. "Huh?"

SpongeBob gasped. The lightbulb that hung above the class science project, Roger, had crackled and burned out. The room was dim.

SpongeBob looked at Patrick. Then he

looked at Roger. Then he looked at Patrick again. If SpongeBob and Patrick didn't act fast, Roger could die!

"I-I-I'm sorry I called you a stupid star!" SpongeBob cried.

"I'm sorry I got you into trouble, and got you moved to the back of the room, and got your Good Noodle star taken away, and threw a book at you, and shot spitballs at you, and . . . ," Patrick babbled anxiously.

"I'm sorry your apology is so long!" SpongeBob interrupted.

"Me too!" said Patrick.

Their eyes locked. "Let's save Roger!" they said at once.

chapter six

"I'll keep Roger warm while you get a lightbulb from the supply closet," SpongeBob instructed Patrick.

"Gotcha! One lightbulb coming right up!" Patrick said as he dashed out of the classroom.

Carefully, SpongeBob reached into the tank and pinched Roger between his thumb and forefinger.

"Don't worry, Roger," he said, "You're in good hands."

First SpongeBob began to rub Roger back and forth against his shirt for warmth.

Then he tried to warm Roger with his breath. He lifted the egg to his mouth. "Ha . . . ha . . . haaaaa," he breathed quickly.

He even tried sitting on Roger. Gently, SpongeBob lowered his backside onto the egg. "Hey, if it works for a hen, why not me?" he wondered aloud. But nothing seemed to work. Roger was cooling fast.

Meanwhile Patrick had finally found the supply closet. A mountain of lightbulb boxes were stacked up to the ceiling.

Instead of taking a lightbulb from a nearby box, Patrick mounted the first box and slowly climbed up the others to reach the lightbulb that was twisted into the ceiling fixture. Once he unscrewed it Patrick rappelled down the boxes to the ground.

"I'm coming, SpongeBob!" Patrick called as he sprinted from the supply closet.

SpongeBob was frantically knitting a scarf for Roger. The clicking of knitting needles could be heard all the way down the hallway. He was knitting so fast the needles were smoking from friction.

"Hurry, Patrick!" SpongeBob cried. "I've got to find Roger some warmth!"

Just then Patrick burst through the door and barreled into the classroom. SpongeBob stood up and ran toward him, cradling Roger in the crook of his arm. Patrick ran towards SpongeBob holding the lightbulb above his head.

Crash! Patrick and SpongeBob collided hard. Both the egg and the lightbulb flew up into the air. SpongeBob and Patrick watched in horror.

"Without the lightbulb Roger will die!" SpongeBob gasped.

"Without Roger the lightbulb will have nothing to warm!" Patrick sobbed.

SpongeBob and Patrick looked at one another. They knew just what to do. They had seen their favorite superheroes, Mermaid Man and Barnacle Boy, do it thousands of times.

At once they crouched down low and then sprang up into the air at the exact same time. SpongeBob stretched his arms up with all of his might. Just as gravity began to tug him back to the ground SpongeBob closed his fingers around the fragile egg.

Patrick was not so lucky. As quickly as he went up, he plummeted down in a heavy heap. He had missed the lightbulb! But as the lightbulb was about to crash onto the floor, Patrick grabbed SpongeBob by his ankles and

thrust him forward. SpongeBob's legs and body shot forward as far as they could go. SpongeBob closed his eyes tightly and stretched his left arm out with determination. The lightbulb landed snugly in his open palm.

SpongeBob opened his eyes and breathed a sigh of relief. "We did it!" he exclaimed. "We saved Roger!"

Patrick gave SpongeBob a tight bear hug. "We're heroes, SpongeBob! Real, live, heroes!"

SpongeBob's face turned red—and then blue. Patrick was hugging him too tightly!

"Can't breathe . . . need air!" SpongeBob squeaked. Patrick loosened his arms and SpongeBob collapsed onto the ground gasping for air.

The two friends walked to the corner of the classroom where Roger's empty tank rested on a crate. SpongeBob placed the egg back in its eggcup.

Patrick stood on a chair and screwed the lightbulb into the socket above. Light filled the room.

Seemingly out of nowhere Mrs. Puff appeared from behind her one-way chalkboard.

"Good job, boys," she said, patting them each on the back. "I saw the whole thing and I couldn't be more proud of your teamwork."

Patrick gave SpongeBob a thumbs-up.

"For your gallant effort to save our class pet, and your enlightened willingness to work together," she said with a wink, "I've decided to award you each one gold star. Although I'm not sure what saving an egg has to do with boating school."

"Woo hooo!" SpongeBob and Patrick yelled and did a victory dance. "Go

SpongeStar, go SpongeStar, go SpongeStar!" Patrick cheered as SpongeBob thrust his hips from side to side.

Suddenly Patrick stopped abruptly. "Wait a minute. Did she just say, 'boating school'?" Patrick asked with disbelief. "I thought this was Spanish class!"

With that Patrick spun on his heel. "See ya, SpongeBob!" he called as he sauntered out of the classroom. "Adios, big, fat meanie!"

And that concluded Patrick Star's first—and last—day of school.

about the author

Jenny Miglis has written more than thirty books for children, including books based on *Blue's Clues, Jimmy Neutron, Rugrats, Bob the Builder, Jay Jay the Jet Plane, Sesame Street,* and *SpongeBob SquarePants.* A former editor of children's books in New York, Jenny is now a freelance writer. She lives in Stavanger, Norway, with her husband, Marius. While she doesn't own a pair of square pants, she does know how to square dance.